We Adopted
a Baby Lamb

For Ila, my magical little tater tot — LJS

Text and illustrations copyright © 2021 by Lori Joy Smith

Tundra Books, an imprint of Penguin Random House Canada Young Readers,
a division of Random House of Canada Limited

Library and Archives Canada Cataloguing in Publication

Title: We adopted a baby lamb / Lori Joy Smith.
Names: Smith, Lori Joy, 1973- author.
Identifiers: Canadiana (print) 2020015348X | Canadiana (ebook) 20200153544 |
ISBN 9780735266537 (hardcover) | ISBN 9780735266544 (EPUB)
Subjects: LCSH: Sheep farming—Juvenile literature. | LCSH: Farm life—Juvenile literature. |
LCSH: Sheep farming—Pictorial works—Juvenile literature. | LCSH: Farm life—Pictorial works—Juvenile literature.
Classification: LCC SF375.2 .S65 2021 | DDC j636.3—dc23

Published simultaneously in the United States of America by Tundra Books of Northern New York,
an imprint of Penguin Random House Canada Young Readers, a division of Random House of Canada Limited

Library of Congress Control Number: 2019956932

All photos © Lori Joy Smith

Acquired by Tara Walker
Edited by Elizabeth Kribs
Designed by John Martz
The artwork in this book was rendered digitally.
The text was set in Smiling Kitten.

Printed and bound in China

www.penguinrandomhouse.ca

1   2   3   4   5   25   24   23   22   21

tundra | Penguin Random House | TUNDRA BOOKS

ori Joy Smith

We Adopted a Baby Lamb

tundra

Hi, my name is Ila, and this is my family. We moved to the country last year because my parents wanted more space and dreamed of a simpler life.

One day we went to visit a two-week-old lamb. He was orphaned and needed a new family. He was so cute that I knew my parents would have to say yes.

When Albert first came home, he was even smaller than our cats! He was too little to live outside in the cold barn, so he stayed in a dog crate in our kitchen.

We knew nothing about caring for a baby lamb. Luckily we have a good friend who grew up on a farm, and she gave us some advice on what supplies we needed.

SUPPLIES for A BABY LAMB

GianT

bag of lamb formula

diapers

thermometer for heating up formula

big baby lamb bottle

LOTS of old blankets and towels

Albert peed on the floor. A LOT.
I tried to make him wear
diapers, but he always wiggled
out of them. (That's why we
needed all the blankets and
towels.)

Noooooo!

diaper

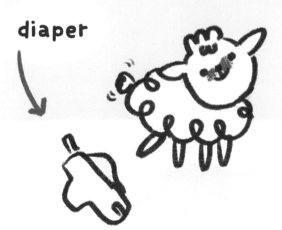

Albert was so cute he even got Sosi to smile. All of a sudden she wasn't as grumpy about our move to the country.

We bought Albert a tiny sweater
so he could play outdoors while
it was cold. He loved wearing it,
even when he was inside. But most
of all, Albert loved blankie time.
(Me too!)

After a few weeks, Albert was big enough to move from the kitchen to a stall in the barn. (I think my mom was tired of cleaning up his poop and pee.)

Even though my dad said he belonged outside, I felt bad about making him sleep out there all alone.

Every night I tucked him into
the barn and wished him sweet
dreams. Every morning I opened
up the barn doors and gave him
his bottle.

Albert grew fast! When he was three months old, it was time to start weaning him. This meant we gave him less formula and he started eating real sheep food.

Albert did NOT like giving up his bottle . . .

But he sure liked food! At first,
it was mostly my mom's tulips.
Next, he discovered dandelions.
Then, apple blossoms — he
couldn't get enough of them!
And, of course, grass.

We found out Albert is part Icelandic sheep. They have lovely flowing locks and are known to be rascals. I have to keep an eye on him. He gets into everything!

Albert loves making new friends,
especially with other animals.
He doesn't seem to notice that
some don't feel the same way
about him.

Friend?

hisssssss

I was worried he was lonely and needed his own flock. The family at a farm down the road brought over a friend for Albert. Monty was big, smelly and his BAAs sounded like burps.

Monty went back that same day.

BAAAAA!

Albert is always happy to see me. You can tell Albert is happy when he hops like a bunny. He also jumps, twirls, spins and loop-the-loops.

I brush his wool and we play chase with Sprout. We do everything together.

But I can't be outside with Albert ALL the time. My mom and dad decided to put up an electric fence so he can stay outside in the field like other sheep. The fence protects him from everything that wants to eat him.

coyotes

foxes

hawks

neighborhood
farm dogs

People told me Albert would end up being just like a pet dog. Instead Sprout started acting like a sheep. I'm starting to act more like a sheep too!

eating
dandelions

Then I realized something.
WE are Albert's flock!
We feed him and play with him
and keep him safe.

Most important of all,
we love him.

Meet Albert!